THE FARMINGTON COMMUNITY LIBRARY
FARMINGTON HILLS BRANCH
32737 WEST TWELVE MILE ROAD
FARMINGTON HILLS, MI 48334-3302
(248) 553-0300

W9-BCW-519

MAY 19 2011

HAPPY BIRTHDAY BAD KITTY

Nick Bruel

A NEAL PORTER BOOK
ROARING BROOK PRESS
NEW YORK

30036010796314

• CONTENTS •

CHAPTER ONE
GOOD MORNING, KITTY! 3

CHAPTER TWO
KITTY'S FIRST YEAR 19

CHAPTER THREE
EVERY PARTY NEEDS DECORATIONS . 33

CHAPTER FOUR
EVERY PARTY NEEDS GUESTS 57

CHAPTER FIVE
WHO STOLE KITTY'S PRESENTS? 83

CHAPTER SIX
EVERY PARTY NEEDS A PIÑATA . . . 101

CHAPTER SEVEN
EVERY PARTY NEEDS CAKE 115

CHAPTER EIGHT
THE PARTY'S OVER 137

CHAPTER NINE
GOOD NIGHT, KITTY 147

APPENDIX 158

•CHAPTER ONE•

GOOD MORNING, KITTY!

GOOD MORNING, KITTY!

Today is going to be a great day! The sun is shining! The birds are singing! Flowers are blooming everywhere with all the colors of the rainbow!

You know what today is, don't you, Kitty? Today is a very special day! Today is the kind of day that only comes once a year! Today is the kind of day that you celebrate ALL day long! Today is the kind of day that deserves a BIG, FUN PARTY!

Now, do you know what today is?

TODAY IS YOUR BIRTHDAY!!!

And that means we start your very special day with a very special **BIRTHDAY BREAKFAST!**

We made all of your favorites . . .

Aardvark **B**agels, **C**lam **D**oughnuts, **E**el **F**ritters, **G**rilled **H**ummingbirds, **I**guana **J**elly, **K**oala **L**emonade, **M**ongoose and **N**uts, **O**rangutan **P**ancakes, **Q**uetzal **R**aisin bread, **S**nake **T**ortillas, **U**nicorn and **V**egetable juice, **W**alrus in **X**O sauce, and for dessert a **Y**ak **Z**abaglione!

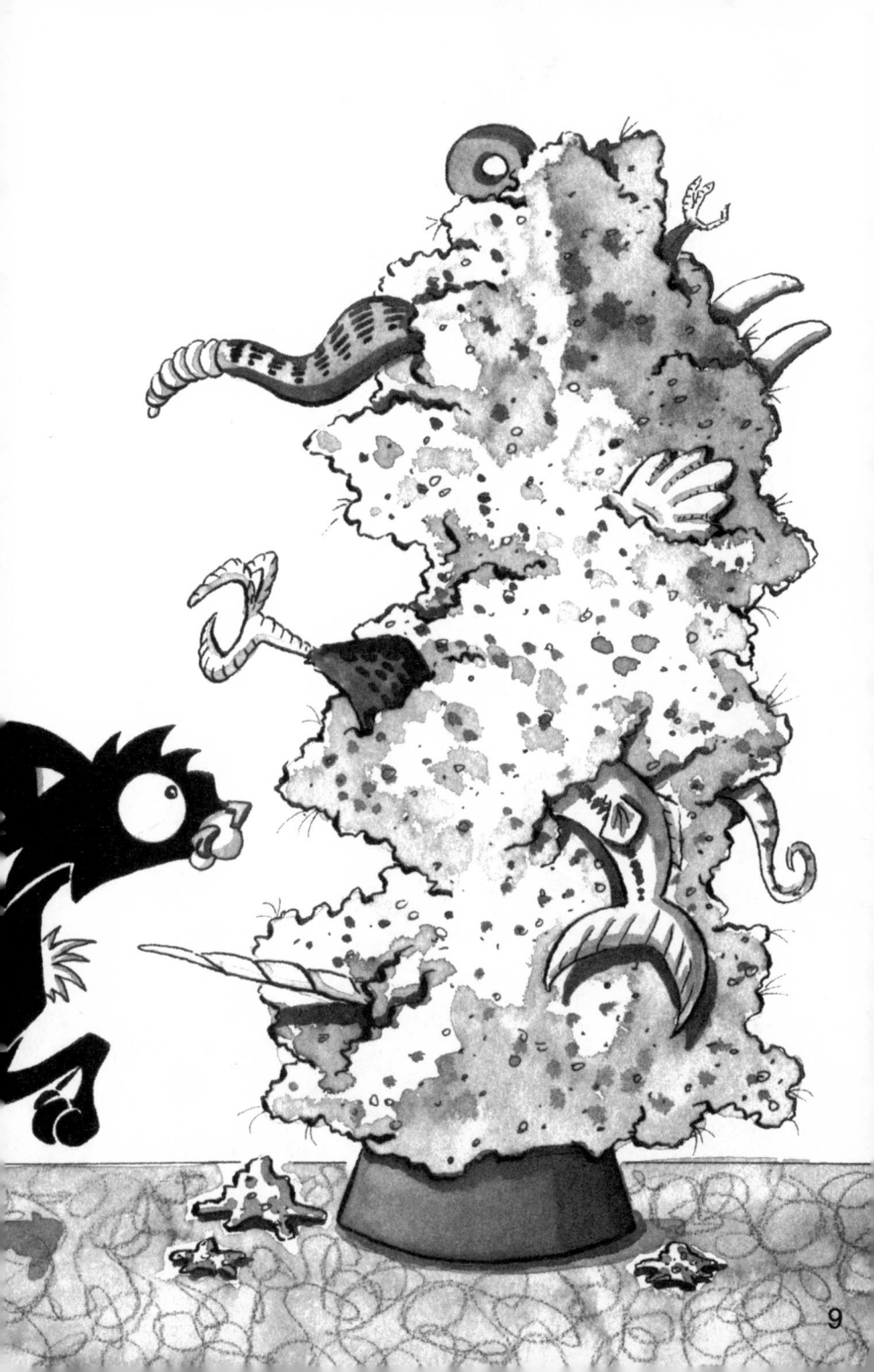

GOBBLE GOBBLE
SLOBBER
MUNCH
GOBBLE SLURP
CHEW CHEW
YUM
SLOBBER
MASTICATE
GULP!
SLURP

ZOOM

BURP
SNORE

Oh, come on, Kitty! You're not going to sleep all day again, are you? All you did yesterday was sleep. All you did the day before yesterday was sleep. And all you did the day before the day before yesterday was sleep.

Are you going to do nothing but sleep every single day?

UNCLE MURRAY'S FUN FACTS

WHY DO CATS SLEEP SO MUCH?

The typical house cat will sleep an average of sixteen hours a day. That's more than TWICE what the average human being sleeps.

One reason cats sleep so much is because they're CREPUSCULAR, which means that they are most active at dawn and at dusk, when the sun is rising and when the sun is setting. Those are the times cats are used to hunting for their food.

Cats are also very light sleepers. Even when they might look like they're sound asleep, all of their senses are still very active. For instance, you can see their ears wiggle and turn while they're sleeping. This way, cats can remain aware of their surroundings even while they sleep and can wake up very quickly if they need to.

Some big cats, like lions, will eat so much after a successful hunt that they will sleep for two straight days afterward. Often it is only the female lions that do the hunting while the male lions do most of the sleeping.

Okay, Kitty. I get it. You're just going to sleep all day again. I guess I'll just decorate the house all by myself. I guess I'll just blow up the balloons all by myself. I guess I'll just let all the guests in all by myself.

I guess I'll just **EAT THE CAKE** and **OPEN THE PRESENTS** all by myself.

Wow. Cats really can wake up quickly.

•CHAPTER TWO•

KITTY'S FIRST YEAR

Before we do anything else, Kitty, it's time for our favorite birthday tradition. It's time to look through the old photo album and remember all of those wonderful days from long ago.

LOOK, KITTY! Here's a picture of you back in the animal shelter where we found you.

Awww! You were SOOOOOOooooo cute!

You were the sweetest, kindest, nicest kitten in the whole shelter. And you were helpful, too!

You used to help keep all of the cages clean. You liked to read to all the other kittens. And you ALWAYS shared your food.

LOOK, KITTY! Here are pictures of your mother!

You and Mama Kitty were very close.

The day eventually came when it was time for you to leave the shelter. That's when you came home to live with us.

But you didn't want to go. You didn't want to leave Mama Kitty, even though you were old enough.

UNCLE MURRAY'S FUN FACTS

WHEN ARE KITTENS OLD ENOUGH TO LEAVE THEIR MOTHERS?

Cats mature much faster than human beings. The typical house cat reaches adulthood when it is only twelve to eighteen months old. Human beings can barely walk at that age!

So when a cat is only twelve weeks old, it is probably old enough to leave its mother and go to a new home. Twelve weeks might seem very young to you and me, but to a cat it is perfectly normal.

1 WEEK OLD

12 WEEKS OLD

1 YEAR OLD

It is very important not to remove a kitten from its mother before it is twelve weeks old.

Kittens learn a lot of important things from their mothers before they're adopted.

They learn how to use the litter box properly.

They learn how to eat solid food.

If you remove a kitten from its mother too early, the kitten might have a more difficult time learning these important lessons from you.

We loved you right away, even though you were sometimes pretty . . . uh . . . grumpy.

Away from your mother, you weren't the same helpful little kitten that we first met. But we still love you.

Although, you don't always make it easy.

•CHAPTER THREE•

EVERY PARTY NEEDS DECORATIONS

Okay, Kitty . . . Let's get started.

The first thing we do is pull out the box of decorations we use every year.

Why don't you help me blow up some balloons.

That's not helping, Kitty.

Okay. Why don't you help me hang some streamers.

That's not helping, Kitty.

Okay, Kitty . . . Why don't you help me put this incredibly delicate and valuable glass birthday vase that's been in my family for a dozen generations onto the mantel.

On second thought, maybe I'll just leave this in the box.

All right, Kitty . . . Since you don't want to help me blow up balloons or hang streamers, will you at least help me to set up the table for all the **PRESENTS** you're going to get?

That's right, Kitty. All I need you to do is help me spread the special birthday party tablecloth onto the table.

Thank you, Kitty. Now you're being helpful.

Gosh! The table looks so festive. Except . . . I think it's missing one little thing, Kitty. What do you think that one little thing is, Kitty?

It's missing **PRESENTS**, of course!

So, I'm going to put one there right now. It's a BIG surprise, Kitty. And I know it's something you REALLY want, Kitty . . . that you really, REALLY, **REALLY** want.

But you have to promise me that you won't open it until the party.

Remember, Kitty . . . You promised not to open the present yet. YOU PROMISED.

MILK
WHINE!
PUPPY CAGE

Where are you going, Kitty? The guests will be here any minute now!

DIG-DIG
RUSTLE

THE GIANT CAT-ALOG OF CAT TOYS
I WANT EVERYTHING!

BE THE MOST POPULAR CAT IN YOUR NEIGHBORHOOD WITH...
THE WORLD'S GREATEST CAT SCRATCHER
Silk cushion stuffed with hummingbird feathers!
Baobab wood base lined with diamonds!

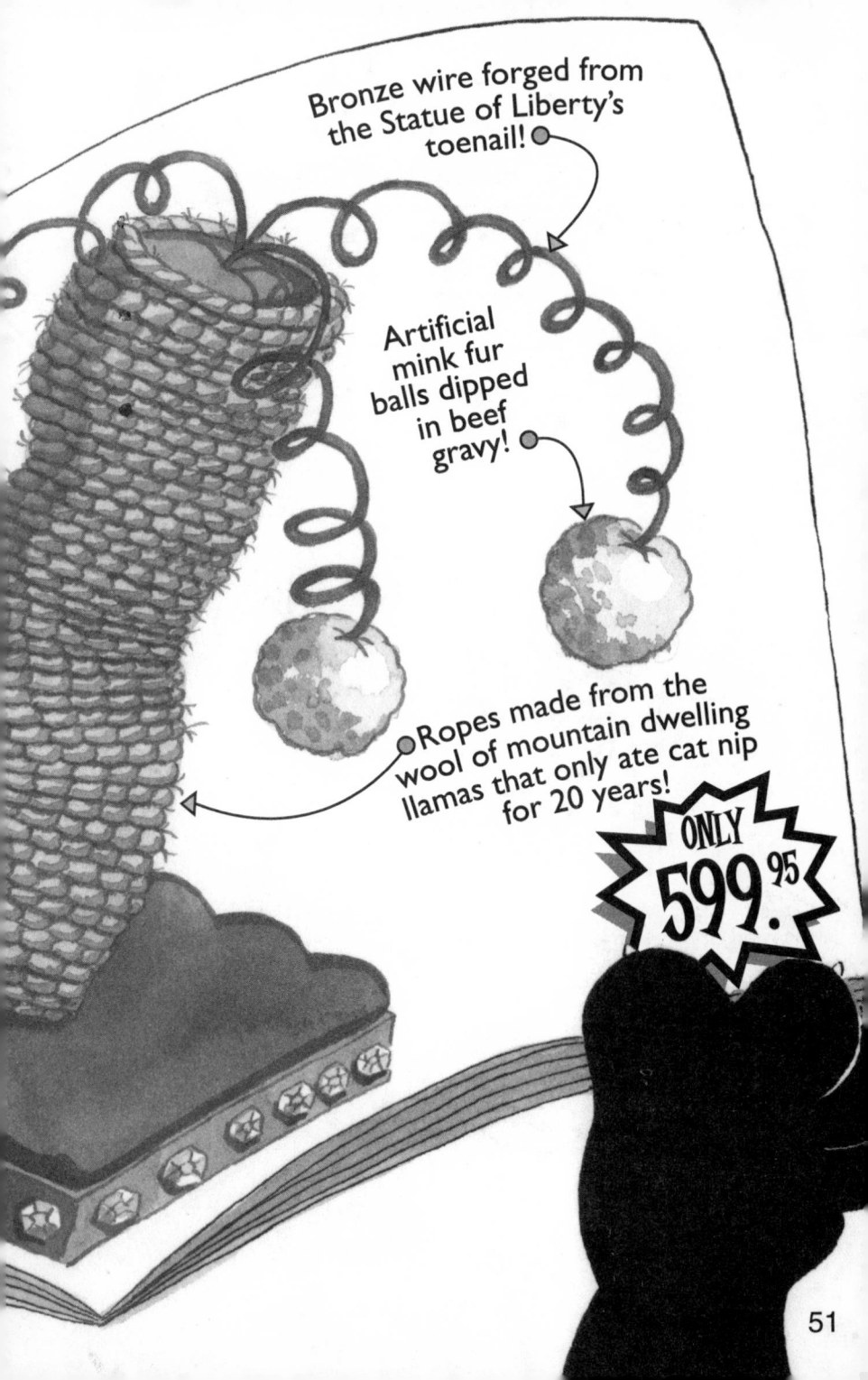
Bronze wire forged from the Statue of Liberty's toenail!
Artificial mink fur balls dipped in beef gravy!
Ropes made from the wool of mountain dwelling llamas that only ate cat nip for 20 years!
ONLY
599.95

UNCLE MURRAY'S FUN FACTS

WHY DO CATS LIKE TO SCRATCH THINGS?

All cats like to scratch things. They'll scratch soft things like chairs or sofas.

They'll scratch hard things like table legs or dressers.

They'll scratch fuzzy things like rugs or carpets.

Cats will scratch just about anything.

Sometimes they'll do it for fun or exercise. But they'll also scratch things because their claws are like our fingernails—they never stop growing. But unlike our fingernails, a cat's claws grows in layers. So cats will sometimes scratch something to rub off an old layer for a newer, fresher, sharper claw layer.

The scratch marks they leave behind are also very important for cats—they mark a cat's territory. Those scratches are territory markers for other cats to both see AND smell. Inside a cat's paw pads are little scent glands that leave little odors on anything they scratch. They act like messages for other cats to read.

GRAB!

DING-DONG!

The guests are here, Kitty! Let's meet them at the door.

•CHAPTER FOUR•

EVERY PARTY NEEDS GUESTS

IT'S BIG KITTY!

Big Kitty is the biggest kitty in the whole neighborhood!

Big Kitty is MUCH bigger than Kitty.

Big Kitty weighs MUCH more than Kitty.

EVERYTHING about Big Kitty is bigger. Even his hair balls are pretty darn big.

I sure hope we have enough birthday cake!

Even Big Kitty's present is BIG! Wow! I wonder what it could be!

Kitty, why don't you open your presents later when . . . Never mind.

Look, Kitty! It's a . . . dead mouse.

I guess it wasn't dead after all.

IT'S THE TWIN KITTIES!

The Twin Kitties are brother and sister and the cutest kitties in the whole neighborhood.

More than anything, they love to PLAY. And they love to play with Kitty!

On those rare occasions when Kitty is not in the mood to play with them . . .

. . . they play with Puppy!

Look, Kitty! They brought you not ONE but TWO presents! I wonder what's in them.

Look, Kitty! It's a ball of string and a ball of twine. How thoughtful.

I'll just put them on the present table where they'll be safe.

IT'S STINKY KITTY!

Stinky Kitty is the—***cough***—stinkiest kitty in the whole—***choke***—neighborhood.

He never brushes his teeth.

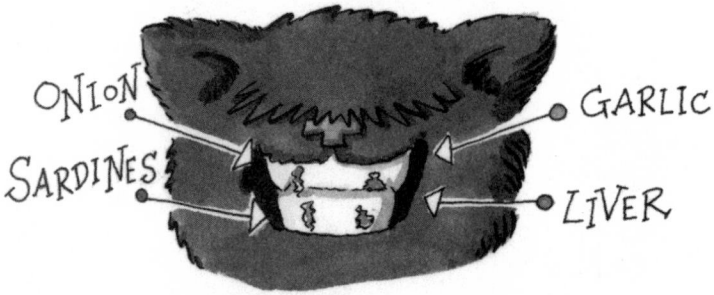

He's always getting dirty.

He likes to sleep in his litter box.

But Stinky Kitty did—***cough***—bring you a very nice-looking present. I wonder what it—***hack***—is!

Look, Kitty! It's an . . . old cardboard paper towel tube.

Oh well, Kitty. It's the thought that counts. Let's put it on the presents table where it will be safe.

IT'S CHATTY KITTY!

*A funny thing happened to me on the way to the party. I saw a stick that was shaped just like a chicken bone only it didn't smell like a chicken bone at all. Mostly, it smelled like a stick. I find that sticks almost never smell like chicken bones unless you were to rub the stick with a chicken bone, but why would you do that?

* Why do you suppose oranges are called "oranges?" Do you think it's because they are colored orange, or is the color orange called "orange" because it's the color of oranges? I wonder why all fruits aren't named after their colors. Grapes could be called "purples" and a bunch of grapes could be called a "bunch of purples," unless they're white grapes, which really aren't white at all but more of a pale green. But you'd still have to be careful because if you asked for a "bunch of purples," someone might give you a big pile of eggplants, which would just be silly, because cats don't eat eggplants. Or grapes. Or oranges either.

Chatty Kitty has brought you such a nice-looking present. Why don't you open it right now! (Do you think I could borrow some of that paper to put in my ears?)

*A moth got into the house the other day, only I wasn't sure if it was a moth or a butterfly because it was big like a butterfly but brown and gray like a moth, and I tried to catch it but it flew too high for me, which is good because some butterflies are poisonous if you eat them, which is gross, but sometimes I can't help myself. It didn't matter, though, because it turned out to be just a feather anyway.

Look, Kitty! It's . . . a collection of old mothballs she found in the closet.

*They also ward off butterflies. **Don't eat them!**

I guess kitties aren't the best gift givers. Oh, well. Let's put them on the table where they'll be safe.

IT'S PRETTY KITTY!

Pretty Kitty is the prettiest kitty in the whole neighborhood.

And she knows it.

She's won over a dozen cat shows.

All of the boy kitties are madly in love with her.

Even the present that Pretty Kitty brought is pretty. It's almost too pretty to . . .

Look, Kitty! It's some tufts of Pretty Kitty's pretty fur.

Oh, Kitty. Don't be like that. It's such pretty fur. That fur has won prizes at cat shows. I'll put it on the present table where it will be safe.

IT'S STRANGE KITTY!

Strange Kitty is the oddest kitty in the whole neighborhood . . . maybe even the whole world. In fact, some people aren't convinced he really is a kitty.

Unlike all of the other kitties, he has no fur.

Unlike all of the other kitties, he wears a hat and necktie.

Unlike all of the other kitties, he would rather sit and read comic books by himself than scratch things or chase mice or sleep all day.

Look, Kitty!
I think Strange
Kitty brought
you a
present, too!

He brought
you a comic
book! Isn't that
nice? Say
"Thank you!"

That's not how we say
"Thank you," Kitty.
It's a very thoughtful
gift. I'll put it on the
present table where
it will be safe.

HEY! Where are all of the other presents I put there?

Where is the comic book Strange Kitty just gave you?

Kitty, did YOU do something with all of the presents?

No?

Well, if you didn't do something with all of your presents, then . . .

•CHAPTER FIVE•

WHO STOLE KITTY'S PRESENTS?

Kitty is certain that another kitty must have stolen all of her presents. After all, who but another kitty would even WANT a cardboard paper towel tube, a ball of string, a ball of twine, a collection of old mothballs, some tufts of cat fur, and an old comic book?

But Kitty thinks there is only one kitty—ONE kitty who could be capable of such a diabolical plot—only ONE kitty could pull off such a hideous crime—only ONE kitty who would rejoice in ruining a perfectly good birthday party by STEALING all of the birthday presents. **AND THAT KITTY IS . . .**

BIG KITTY

HEIGHT: Very, very tall.

WEIGHT: Weighs about the same as a large cinder block.

LAST SEEN: Eating ten pounds of sausages.

Only Big Kitty is big and strong enough to carry all of those presents home!

That's where he will play with them all by himself while laughing—LAUGHING—at Kitty.

But Big Kitty doesn't have the presents!
So the guilty kitty must be . . .

THE TWIN KITTIES

EYES: Like four cute little yellow gumdrops.

NOSES: Like a pair of cute little red buttons.

LAST SEEN: Doing just the cutest little things. I swear, your heart would have just melted if you'd seen it. They are just so darling!

It would have been easy for one of them to stand guard while the other one stole all of the presents!

They will add the presents to their own massive collection of toys from which they will build a mountain so that they can look down at Kitty and laugh—LAUGH!

But the Twin Kitties don't have the presents!

So the guilty kitty must be . . .

STINKY KITTY

EYES: No one—***cough***—dares get close enough to find out.

FUR: Dark gray. But might really be white.

LAST SEEN: Rummaging through the—***hack***—dumpster behind the fish market.

Stinky Kitty probably used his horrendous odor to distract everyone while he stole the presents!

Then he'll bury them in his litter box where no one would ever look and survive to tell the story. And then he will laugh—LAUGH!

But Stinky Kitty doesn't have the presents!

So the guilty kitty must be . . .

CHATTY KITTY

EYES: What?

FUR: Huh? What? Say that again.

FUR: How's that?

LAST SEEN: Sorry. I just can't hear you.

* Maybe all of your presents rolled under the sofa. That happens to me all the time. Once I found a crumpled-up piece of paper and was playing with it until it rolled under the sofa. I waited for a while, but it didn't come back out until one day someone moved the sofa to clean under it and there was the paper, so I played

She must have stolen the MEOW

MEOW MEOW MEOW

PRETTY KITTY

EYES: Like a pair of deep blue lakes at dawn's light.
FUR: Like a field of freshly fallen snow on a crisp winter's day.
LAST SEEN: Winning first prize at a DOG show—she is THAT pretty.

It must have been Pretty Kitty. Because she's jealous.

She was probably jealous because none of the presents were for her.

So she's going to make all of the boy kitties carry the presents back to her place. And then she will laugh—LAUGH—**LAUGH!**

But Pretty Kitty doesn't have the presents!
So the guilty kitty must be . . .

STRANGE KITTY

FUR: None.
HAT: Black.
LAST SEEN: At a comic-book convention debating about which underwater superhero was most powerful: Captain Poseidon or Mudskipper Lass.

Strange Kitty is a big weirdo. Not only is he the only kitty left, he's DIFFERENT. He must be the guilty kitty!

He probably took all of the presents and hid them under his hat. He probably has all of the stolen presents under his hat RIGHT NOW!

Strange Kitty is such an oddball. He's always pretending to be something he's not . . .

. . . like a superhero.

. . . or a swash-buckling pirate.

HE TOOK HIS VORPAL SWORD IN HAND...
. . . or a brave dragon slayer.
. . . or a famous Broadway dancer.
GOTTA DANCE!
He is such a strange kitty.
MEOW MEOW
WASN'T ME.

Well, if Strange Kitty didn't take the presents, then who did? This is quite a mystery.

Puppy? Is that a piece of string caught on your ear? Is that a tuft of Pretty Kitty's fur stuck on your forehead? Is that an old mothball sticking out from between your toes?

Uh-oh.

•CHAPTER SIX•

EVERY PARTY NEEDS A PIÑATA

RUN, PUPPY, RUN!

They think you stole Kitty's presents!

(Did you?)

MEOW
MEOW
MEOW

KITTIES! KITTIES! PLEASE!

I'm sure Puppy has a very good explanation.

(Don't you?)

BIG BOOK OF ROBOTS
MIGHTY DOG

OH NO!

Puppy is all tangled up in electrical cords and speaker wires!

COOL!
MELVIN COMICS

EGADS!

What do you naughty kitties think you're doing with Puppy?

WHOA!
NICE!
SUPER-WORM

JUMPIN' JEHOSHAPHAT!
The kitties want to use Puppy as a piñata!

MEOW
MEOW
MEOW
DO YOU HAVE ANY "MEGA MOUSE?"
YUP.
THE RED BIRD

NO, KITTIES, NO!

Puppy does not have candy inside of him! I swear!

Something must be done or Puppy could get hurt. But what can we do?

WAIT! I know . . .

What three words can bring peace to all nations? What three words can create order out of chaos? What three words can soothe the savage instincts of a bunch of kitties that have lost all control?

MEOW MEOW
WHEN DID HE GET FREEZE VISION?
ISSUE #152.
MEGA MOUSE

WHO WANTS CAKE?!

•CHAPTER SEVEN•

EVERY PARTY NEEDS CAKE

That's right, Kitties. Because this is a very special birthday, we have a very special birthday cake. It's made out of all of your favorite foods!

IG KITTY LOVES ARDINES
STINKY KITTY LOVES LIMBURGER CHEESE
SUPERHERO TRADING CARDS FOR STRANGE KITTY
WHO'S YOUR FAVORITE MEMBER?
THE PHENOMENAL TUSK!
MEGAN

And the icing is made out of Kitty's very favorite food! Liver!

What's wrong, Kitty? Don't you like your cake?

Kitty, are you upset because it's not a CHOCOLATE cake? I know you wanted a chocolate cake, but I already explained to you why you can NEVER have a chocolate cake.

Sorry.

UNCLE MURRAY'S FUN FACTS

WHY IS CHOCOLATE BAD FOR CATS?

If you offer a cat some chocolate, she'll probably eat it. If you offer a cat some chocolate cake, she'll probably eat it.

But chocolate is like POISON to cats! So never offer it to them!

Chocolate contains a chemical compound called THEOBROMINE that is harmless to human beings but very dangerous for cats.

If a cat eats chocolate, she can become very sick and, yes, maybe even die.

So it's very important that you never leave chocolate lying around that a cat might eat by accident.

And the same goes for dogs and most birds. It's very important to keep chocolate away from all of your pets at home.

Uh-oh. Kitty is starting to lose her temper. We better do something FAST.

Kitty! Don't tell me you've forgotten about the **BIG PRESENT** I gave you this morning! Don't you want to open it now?!

I know this is something you've been wanting for a very long time! Well, your wait is finally over, because you now have your very own . . .

BIG WINTER SWEATER!
And it looks just adorable on you.

HAVE YOU READ THE ONE WHERE THE SLAB EATS THE MOON?
NO WAY! COOL!

Oh no! The sweater didn't work! I don't understand why! And I think Kitty is about to lose it if we don't do something right away.

WAIT! I almost forgot!

Look, Kitty! I almost forgot to give you one last present. It's even better than a big winter sweater! It's . . .

A MATCHING HAT AND BOOTIES!

Don't you just love them, Kitty? And they fit you perfectly! The nice lady at the cat sweater store told me they don't make this pattern anymore. No other kitty in the whole world owns this sweater and this hat and these booties.

Aren't you **LUCKY?!**

Now, wait here while I go get the camera. This will make a great Christmas card. Then everyone we know will see just how very, very cute you look!

Kitty?

Are you okay, Kitty?

Uh-oh.

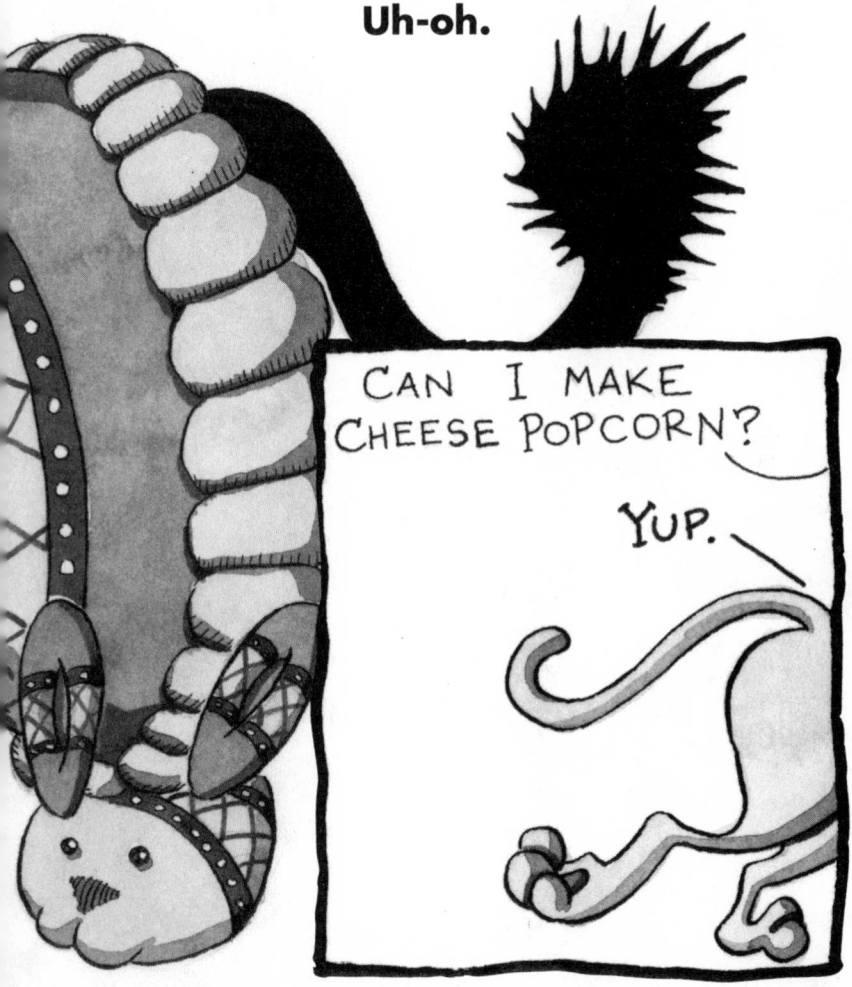

RUN FOR YOUR LIVES!

Kitty's having a major freak-out!

* MEOW!
MEOW!
MEOW!

We woke her up when all she wanted was to sleep!

She didn't get the gifts she wanted
And most of the gifts she did get
are still missing!

She
didn't
like the
balloons
or the
decoration

She didn't get to hit the piñata!

She didn't even get the cake she wanted!

Head for the door, kitties! And don't stop until you're safe at home!

Thanks for coming, kitties. I hope you had a good time. See you next year!

•CHAPTER EIGHT•

THE PARTY'S OVER

Well, Kitty . . . I hope you're happy.

The decorations are ruined. The cake is ruined. Your new sweater is ruined. And all of your party guests have fled the house, running for their lives.

Just like last year. And the year before that. And the year before that. *Sigh*

You know what, Kitty? Sometimes . . . just sometimes . . . you are a truly **BAD KITTY**.

DING-
DONG!

MEOW MEOW HISS
SPIT MEOW
HISS MEOW FFT
FFT HISS MEOW
MEOW SPIT FFT
MEOW
HISS

Oh, hush, Kitty. It's probably just one of the other kitties coming back because she forgot something.

Or maybe not.

Maybe it's a nice surprise for you.

Why don't you open the door to find out.

MEOW?
LICK

Well, Kitty. I guess you got what you wanted for your birthday after all.

•CHAPTER NINE•

GOOD NIGHT, KITTY

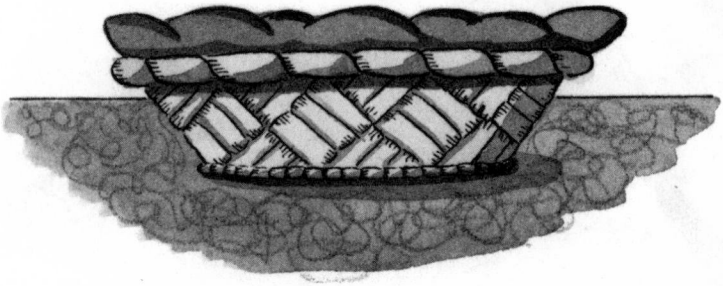

Good-bye, Mama Kitty. It was good seeing you again.

Maybe Kitty and I will go visit YOU someday.

What a fun day this has been, Kitty. Wasn't it great to see Mama Kitty again? Weren't all of those balloons and streamers just lovely before you destroyed, demolished, decimated, and shredded them all? Wasn't it great to see all of your friends again, even though you did chase them out of the house when you went berserk? Wasn't that a beautiful cake you sprayed on the walls?

Well, the day's not over yet, Kitty! There's one more surprise left for you on your birthday! Puppy worked very hard to make something extra special for you.

Look, Kitty! It's . . .

THE WORLD'S WORST CAT SCRATCHER!
CARDBOARD PAPER TOWEL TUBE
OLD COMIC BOOK

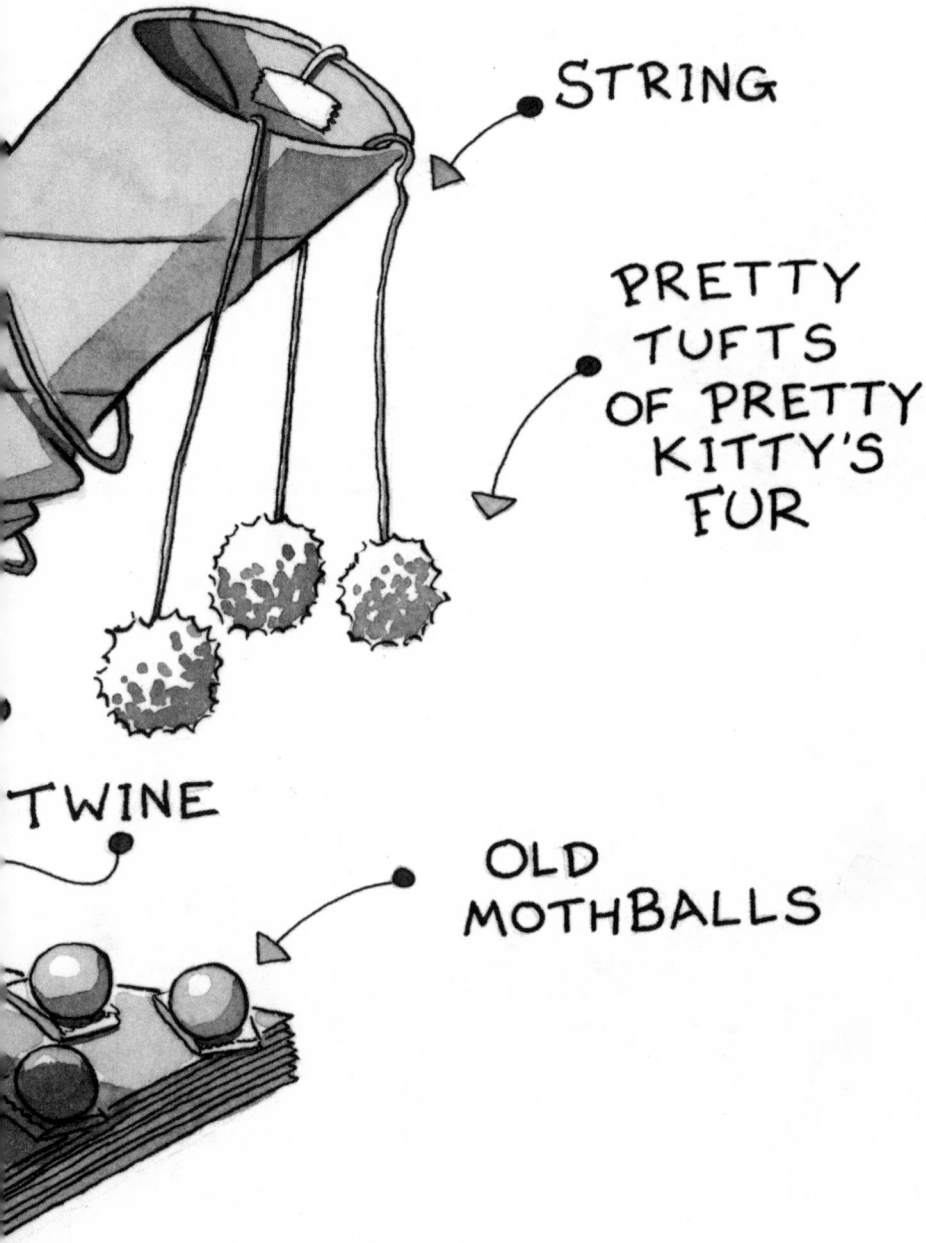
STRING
PRETTY TUFTS OF PRETTY KITTY'S FUR
TWINE
OLD MOTHBALLS

SCRATCH

TREMBLE

POOF!

SLURP!

Good night, Kitty.

• APPENDIX •

What Was That Kitty's Breed?

Even though all domestic cats, or house cats, are the sam species, different characteristics like behavior and appearanc separate one type of cat from another. Each of the kitties th came to the birthday party represented a different breed of co

Big Kitty is a Maine coon cat, one of th largest cat breeds. The males can weigh a much as eighteen pounds. They derived the name Coon cats because their long hair ar bushy, striped tails make them resemble ra coons. Some people think the first Maine coo Cat came from a group of six pet cats sent to Maine by Mar Antoinette when she was planning to escape from France du ing the French Revolution.

The Twin Kitties are American shorthair ca American shorthairs come in a variety of eigh different colors and patterns. Though they a called American shorthairs, the first ones can from Europe with early settlers. There are eve records that show they were on the *Mayflowe*

Stinky Kitty is a Persian cat, the number o breed in popularity thanks to their easygoi personality. Although Persians aren't known be any stinkier than other breeds of cats, th do require daily combings of their dense, lo

r and even occasional baths. Because their legs are short, ey don't jump very high. But they do like to run.

Chatty Kitty is a Siamese cat, a breed that originated in Thailand, but back in the 1800s Thailand was known as Siam. Siamese cats are considered one of the oldest breeds. Many other breeds such as the Burmese and the ocicat have been derived from the Siamese. And, es, they are well known for being . . . talkative.

Pretty Kitty is a Turkish Angora cat, a breed that originated in the mountainous regions of Turkey where a long, thick coat of fur would be useful during their harsh winters. The Turkish Angora is considered such a national treasure that in 1917 the government of Turkey and the nkara Zoo began a program that continues to this day to reserve the breed.

Strange Kitty is a sphynx cat, a natural mutation that was first seen in Toronto, Canada, in 1966. Most sphynx cats have absolutely no fur on their bodies except for a very fine fuzz, and they may not even have whiskers. This means that if they sit under the sun too ong, they can actually get a sunburn. Because their skin is nprotected by fur, they need to take baths at least once a week.

In memory of Sam and Hercules,
Zou-zou, Halloween, Tom, Lucky, Choo-choo,
and all of my other pets I have loved and not forgotten

Copyright © 2009 by Nick Bruel
A Neal Porter Book
Published by Roaring Brook Press
Roaring Brook Press is a division of Holtzbrinck Publishing Holdings Limited Partnership
175 Fifth Avenue, New York, New York 10010
www.roaringbrookpress.com
All rights reserved

Distributed in Canada by H.B. Fenn and Company Ltd.

Cataloging-in-Publication Data is on file at the Library of Congress.
ISBN: 978-1-59643-342-7

Roaring Brook Press books are available for special promotions and premiums.
For details contact: Director of Special Markets, Holtzbrinck Publishers.

First Edition September 2009
Printed in April 2010 in the United States of America by RR Donnelley, Harrisonburg, Virginia
5 7 9 10 8 6

Want more Bad Kitty?
Read the hilarious companion book to *Happy Birthday, Bad Kitty.*

★ "Multiple copies are a must."
—*Kirkus*, starred review

★ "[Readers] will all be equally anxious to sink their claws into this giddy offering."
—*Bulletin for the Center of Children's Books*, starred review

Available in hardcover ISBN 978-1-59643-341-0
and paperback ISBN 978-0-312-58138-1